MONTY + SYLVESTER

A TALE OF EVERYDAY SUPER HEROES

BY

CARLY GLEDHILL

FOR NICK – C.G.

ORCHARD BOOKS

First published in Great Britain in 2018 by
The Watts Publishing Group
This edition first published in 2018

1 3 5 7 9 10 8 6 4 2

Text and illustrations © Carly Gledhill, 2018

A CIP catalogue record for this book is available
from the British Library.

HB ISBN 978 1 40835 174 1
PB ISBN 978 1 40835 175 8

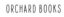

MIX
Paper from
responsible sources
FSC® C104740

Printed and bound in China

Orchard Books
An imprint of Hachette Children's Group
Part of The Watts Publishing Group Limited
Carmelite House, 50 Victoria Embankment
London EC4Y 0DZ

An Hachette UK Company
www.hachette.co.uk

www.hachettechildrens.co.uk

MONTY + SYLVESTER

A TALE OF EVERYDAY SUPER HEROES

CARLY GLEDHILL

YEAH!

ORCHARD

MEET MONTY AND SYLVESTER.
THEY'RE SUPER HEROES (IN TRAINING).

MONTY IS READING
THE SUPER HERO MANUAL.

SYLVESTER IS WORKING OUT.

1 2 3 Ouch 4 Ouch 5 Ouch

PUSH UPS →

FOUR IMPORTANT STEPS TO BECOMING A SUPER HERO

(TAKEN FROM THE MANUAL)

STEP 1
STAR JUMPING

INVISIBLE PANTS READY!

STEP 2
RESEARCHING

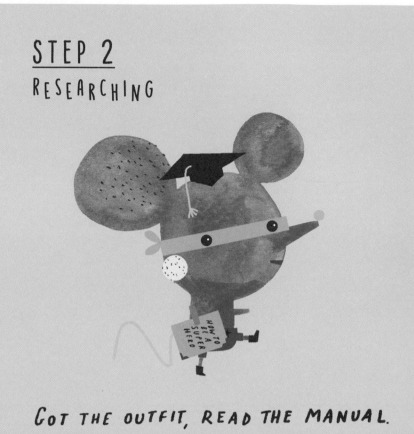

GOT THE OUTFIT, READ THE MANUAL.

STEP 3
LUNGING

MASK TO HIDE IDENTITY

STEP 4
SELF DEFENCE

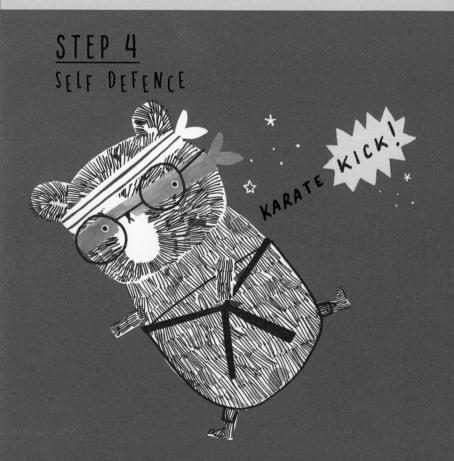

KARATE KICK!

AFTER ALL THAT PRACTICE IT'S TIME TO GO
OUT AND **SAVE THE WORLD**...

... IF ANYONE
NEEDS THEM TO.

TUMBLEWEED →

THE PHONE IS RINGING. THIS MEANS **SOMEBODY NEEDS HELP!**

IT'S TIME.

AWAY THEY BRAVELY GO.

IT'S A CLASSIC. STUBBORN CAT, STUCK UP A TREE.

BUT THERE IS NOTHING WRITTEN IN THE MANUAL ABOUT THIS,
WHAT ARE THEY GOING TO DO?

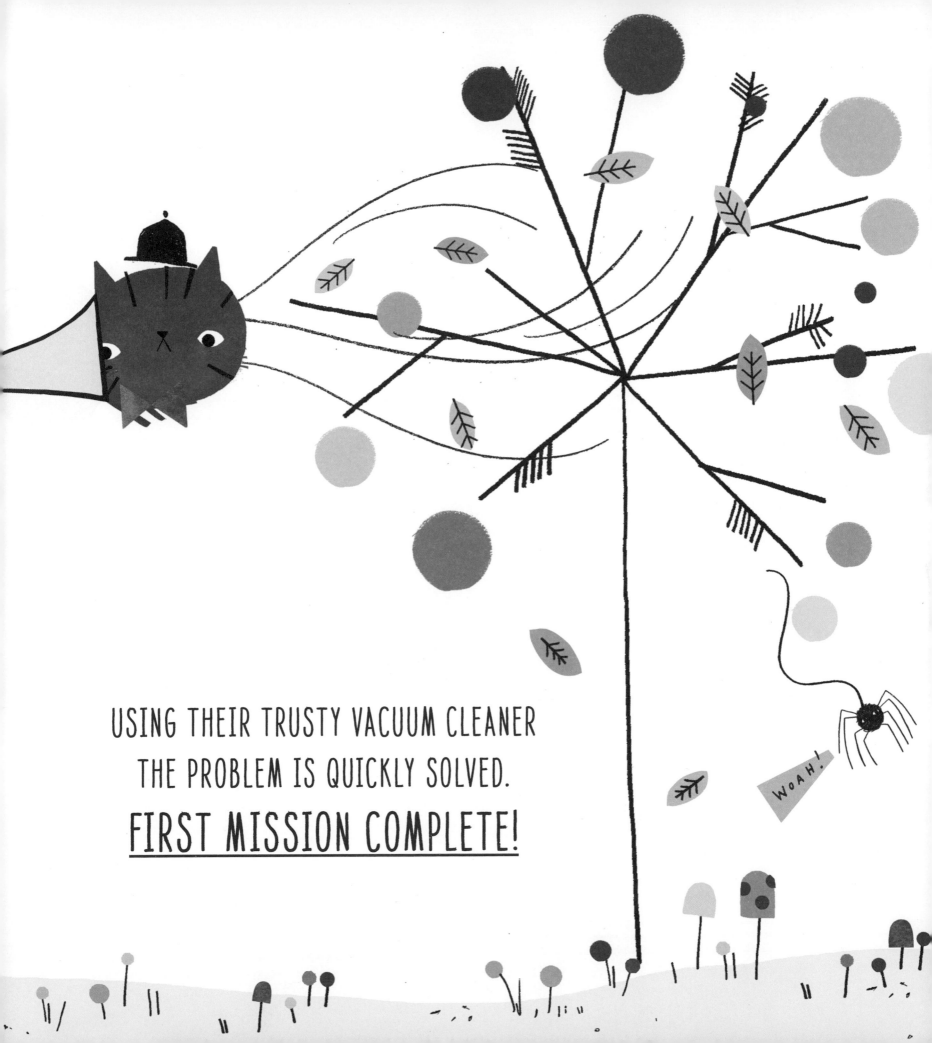

USING THEIR TRUSTY VACUUM CLEANER
THE PROBLEM IS QUICKLY SOLVED.
FIRST MISSION COMPLETE!

WOAH!

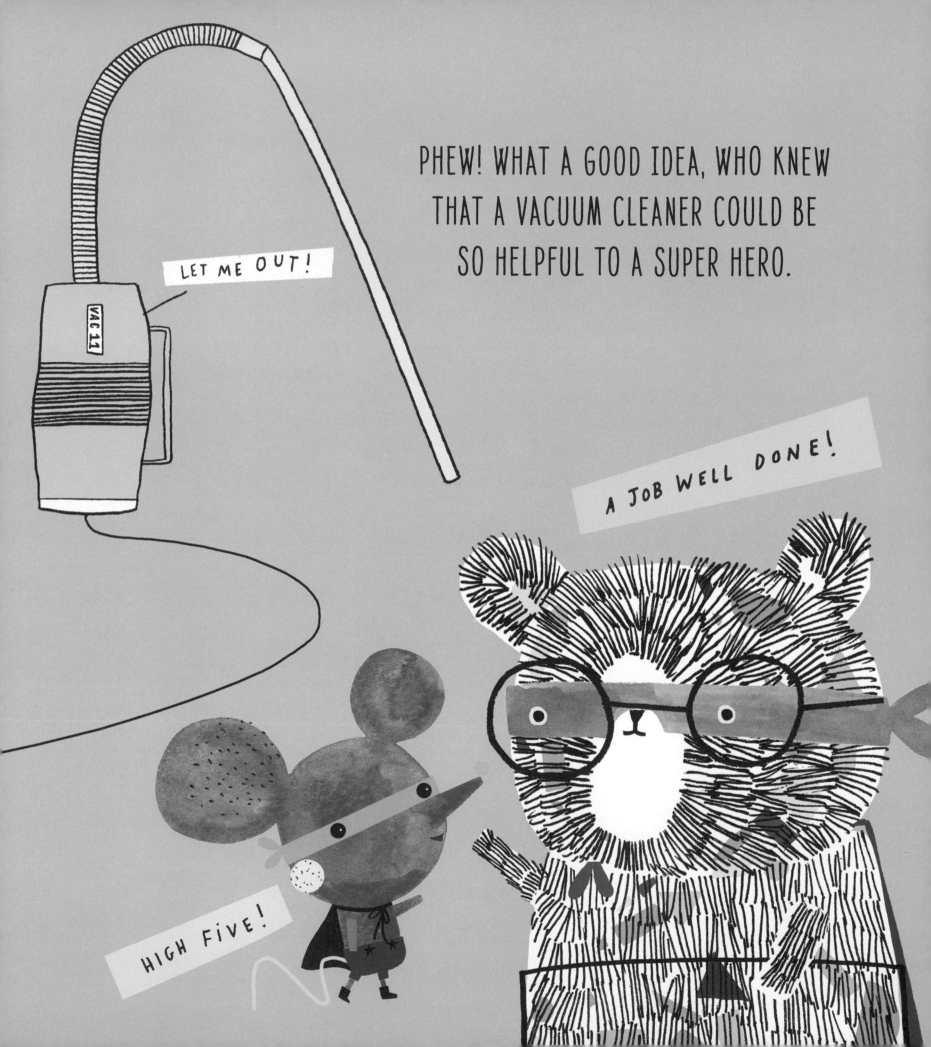

PHEW! WHAT A GOOD IDEA, WHO KNEW THAT A VACUUM CLEANER COULD BE SO HELPFUL TO A SUPER HERO.

THE PHONE IS RINGING AGAIN,
IT'S TIME FOR THE
NEXT MISSION!

THE VACUUM CLEANER IS REALLY HELPING.

NO VILLAIN IS A MATCH FOR MONTY AND SYLVESTER.

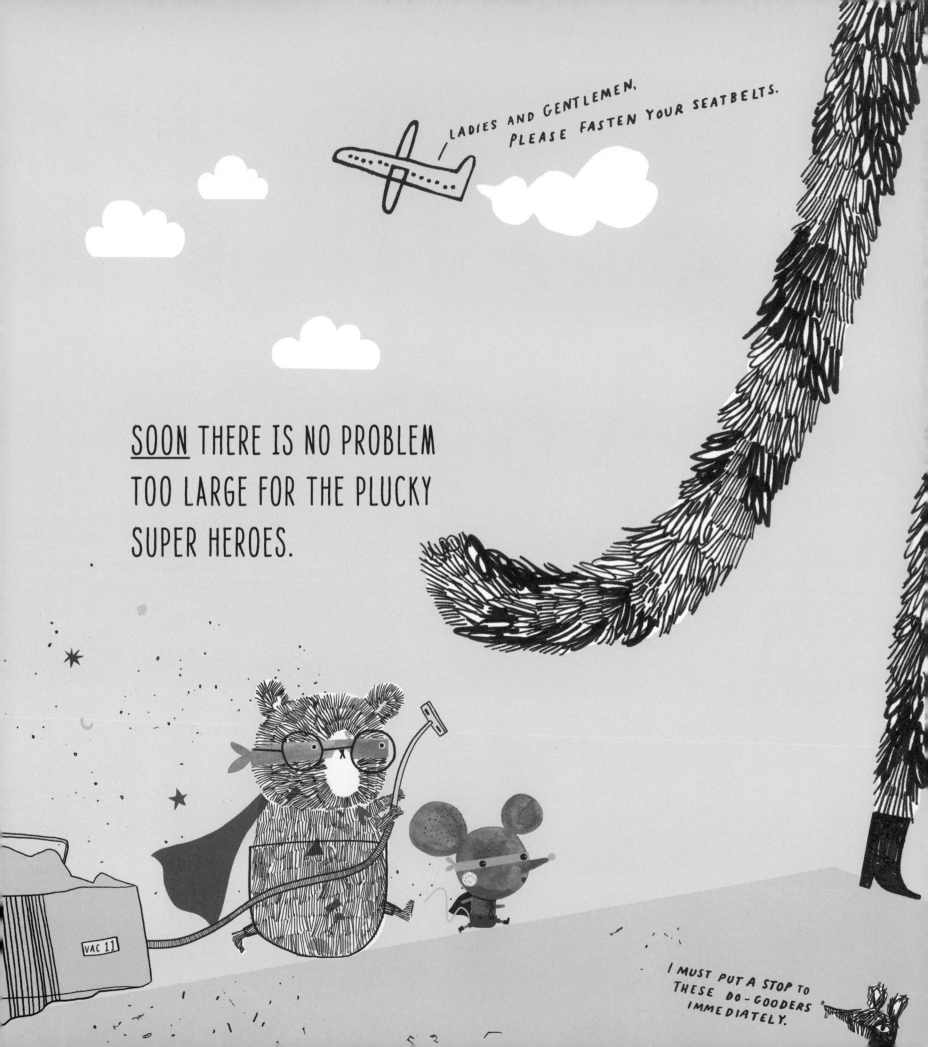

LADIES AND GENTLEMEN, PLEASE FASTEN YOUR SEATBELTS.

SOON THERE IS NO PROBLEM TOO LARGE FOR THE PLUCKY SUPER HEROES.

VAC 11

I MUST PUT A STOP TO THESE DO-GOODERS IMMEDIATELY.

CHARMING. I DON'T LIKE BEARS ANYWAY.

IT IS ALL GOING SO WELL UNTIL...

I'M FREE!

YOU THINK YOU'RE SO CLEVER BUT YOU'RE NOT! YOU CAN'T RELY ON A VACUUM CLEANER TO DO YOUR DIRTY WORK. I'M IN CHARGE NOW AND YOU HAVE TO STOP!

TWO, BUFFOONS!

EVIL SPOTLIGHT

OH DEAR, THIS DOESN'T LOOK GOOD.
HOW ARE THEY POSSIBLY GOING TO ESCAPE?

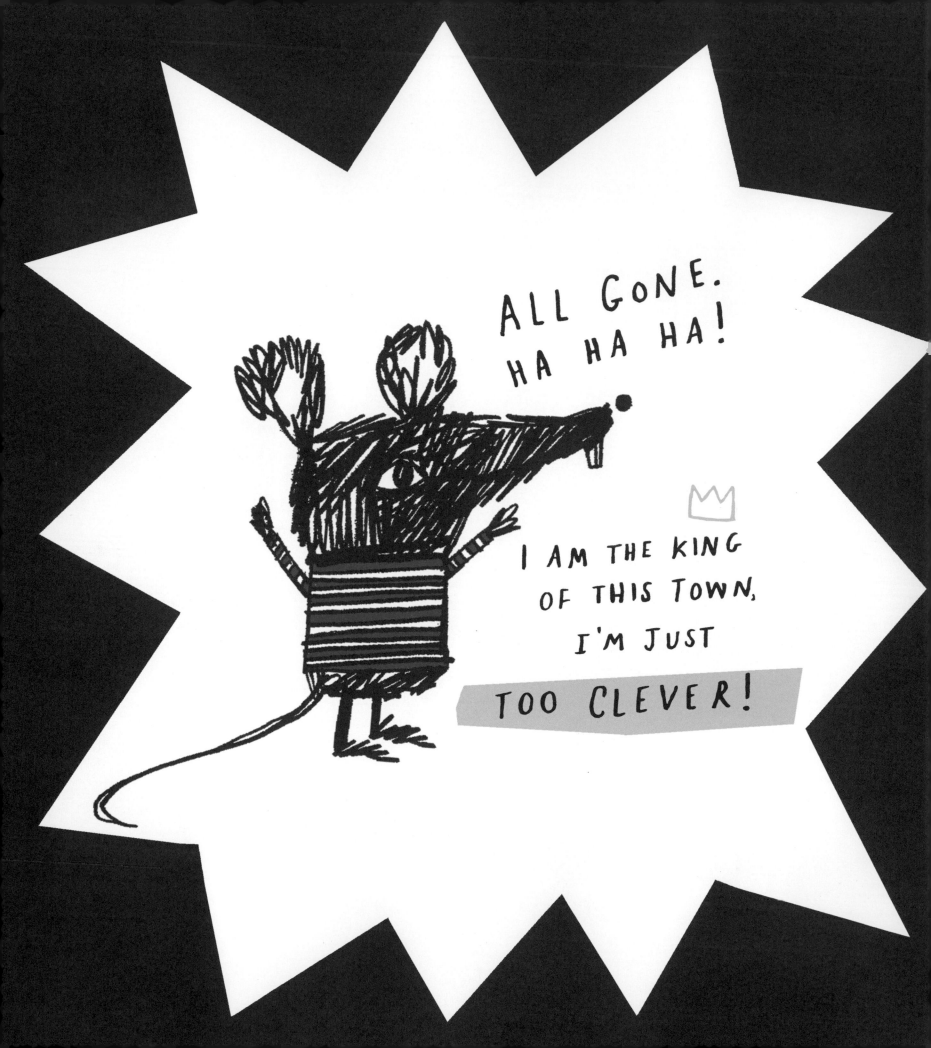

THAT'S THAT THEN. THE BAD GUY WON.

HOORAY!

POW POW POW!

...BECAUSE THE NEXT TIME THE RED PHONE SOUNDED THEY WOULD HAVE <u>A FEW EXTRA HELPERS!</u>

A TOPNOTCH JOB WELL DONE.
MISSION COMPLETE!
TIME TO PUT THEIR
FEET UP, WATCH TV,
EAT SOME CAKE...

TO DO:
BECOME SUPER HEROES ✓
CAPTURE BAD GUY ✓
SAVE WORLD ✓

...WAIT A SECOND.

YOU NEED US

WHERE?